THE ULTIMATE MINECRAFT COMIC BOOK

BY

ZACK ZOMBIE COMICS

VOLUME 1

THE CURSE OF HEROBRINE

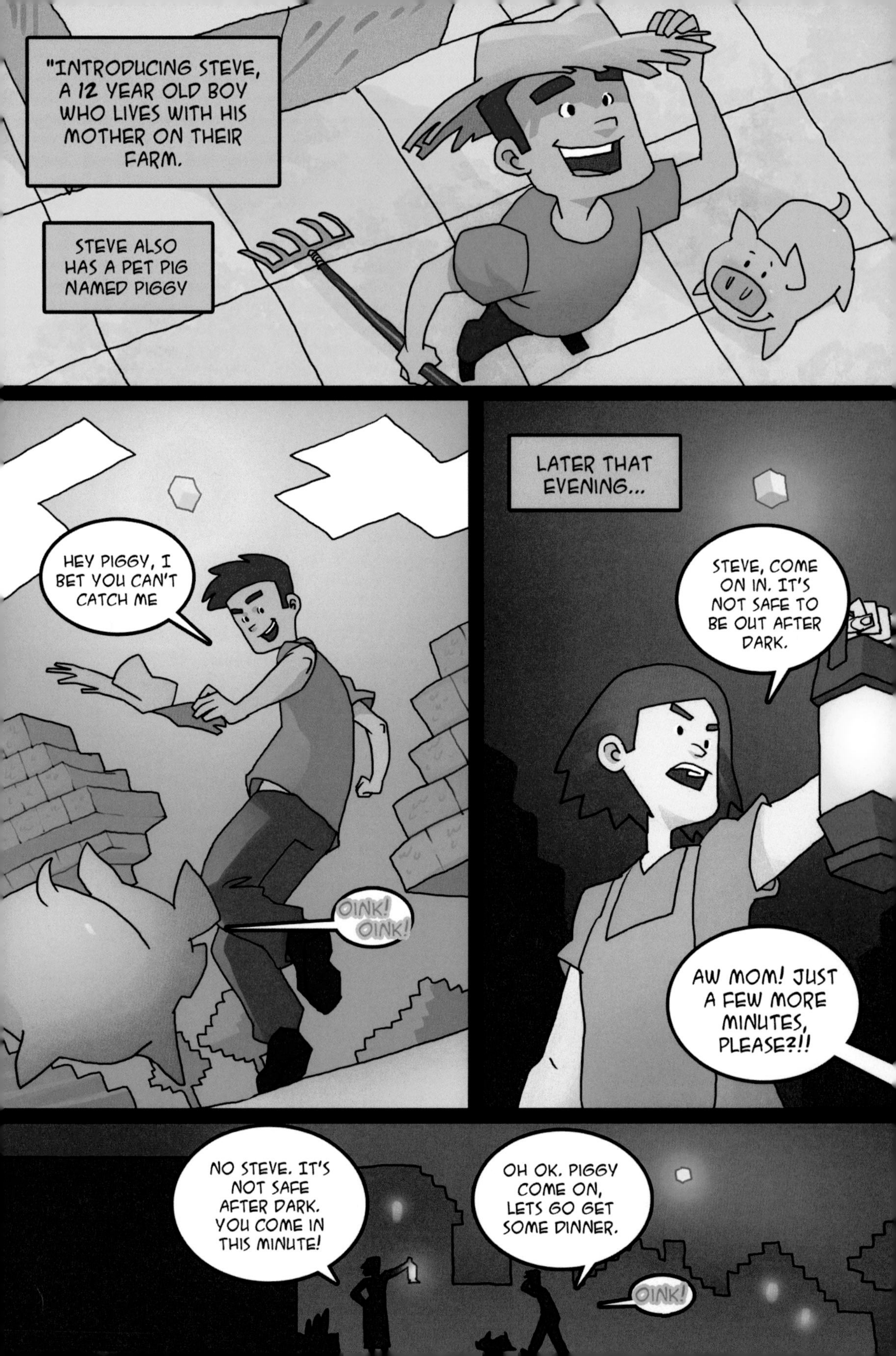
"INTRODUCING STEVE, A 12 YEAR OLD BOY WHO LIVES WITH HIS MOTHER ON THEIR FARM.
STEVE ALSO HAS A PET PIG NAMED PIGGY
HEY PIGGY, I BET YOU CAN'T CATCH ME
OINK! OINK!
LATER THAT EVENING...
STEVE, COME ON IN. IT'S NOT SAFE TO BE OUT AFTER DARK.
AW MOM! JUST A FEW MORE MINUTES, PLEASE?!!
NO STEVE. IT'S NOT SAFE AFTER DARK. YOU COME IN THIS MINUTE!
OH OK. PIGGY COME ON, LETS GO GET SOME DINNER.
OINK!

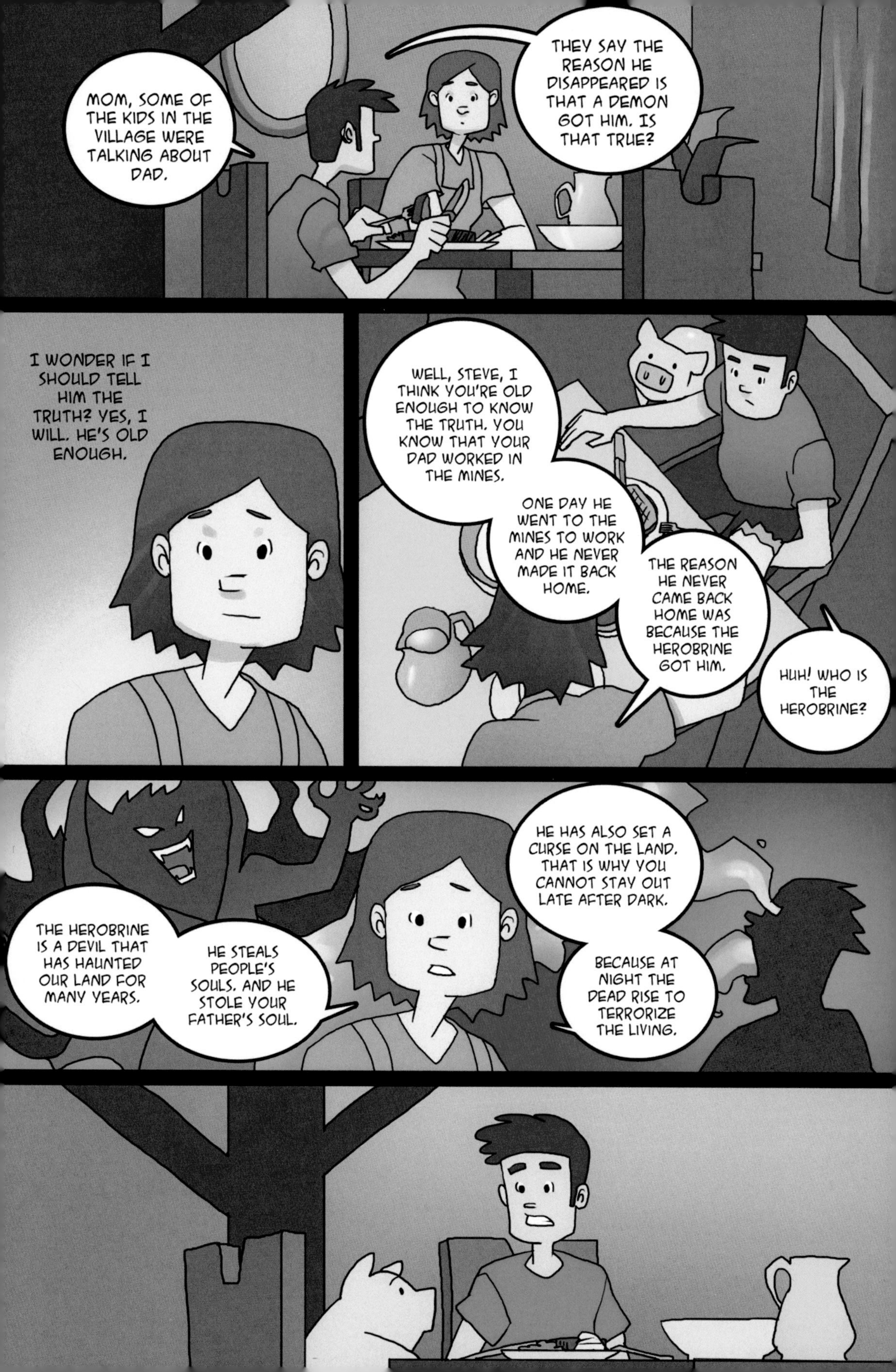
MOM, SOME OF THE KIDS IN THE VILLAGE WERE TALKING ABOUT DAD.
THEY SAY THE REASON HE DISAPPEARED IS THAT A DEMON GOT HIM. IS THAT TRUE?
I WONDER IF I SHOULD TELL HIM THE TRUTH? YES, I WILL. HE'S OLD ENOUGH.
WELL, STEVE, I THINK YOU'RE OLD ENOUGH TO KNOW THE TRUTH. YOU KNOW THAT YOUR DAD WORKED IN THE MINES.
ONE DAY HE WENT TO THE MINES TO WORK AND HE NEVER MADE IT BACK HOME.
THE REASON HE NEVER CAME BACK HOME WAS BECAUSE THE HEROBRINE GOT HIM.
HUH! WHO IS THE HEROBRINE?
THE HEROBRINE IS A DEVIL THAT HAS HAUNTED OUR LAND FOR MANY YEARS.
HE STEALS PEOPLE'S SOULS. AND HE STOLE YOUR FATHER'S SOUL.
HE HAS ALSO SET A CURSE ON THE LAND. THAT IS WHY YOU CANNOT STAY OUT LATE AFTER DARK.
BECAUSE AT NIGHT THE DEAD RISE TO TERRORIZE THE LIVING.

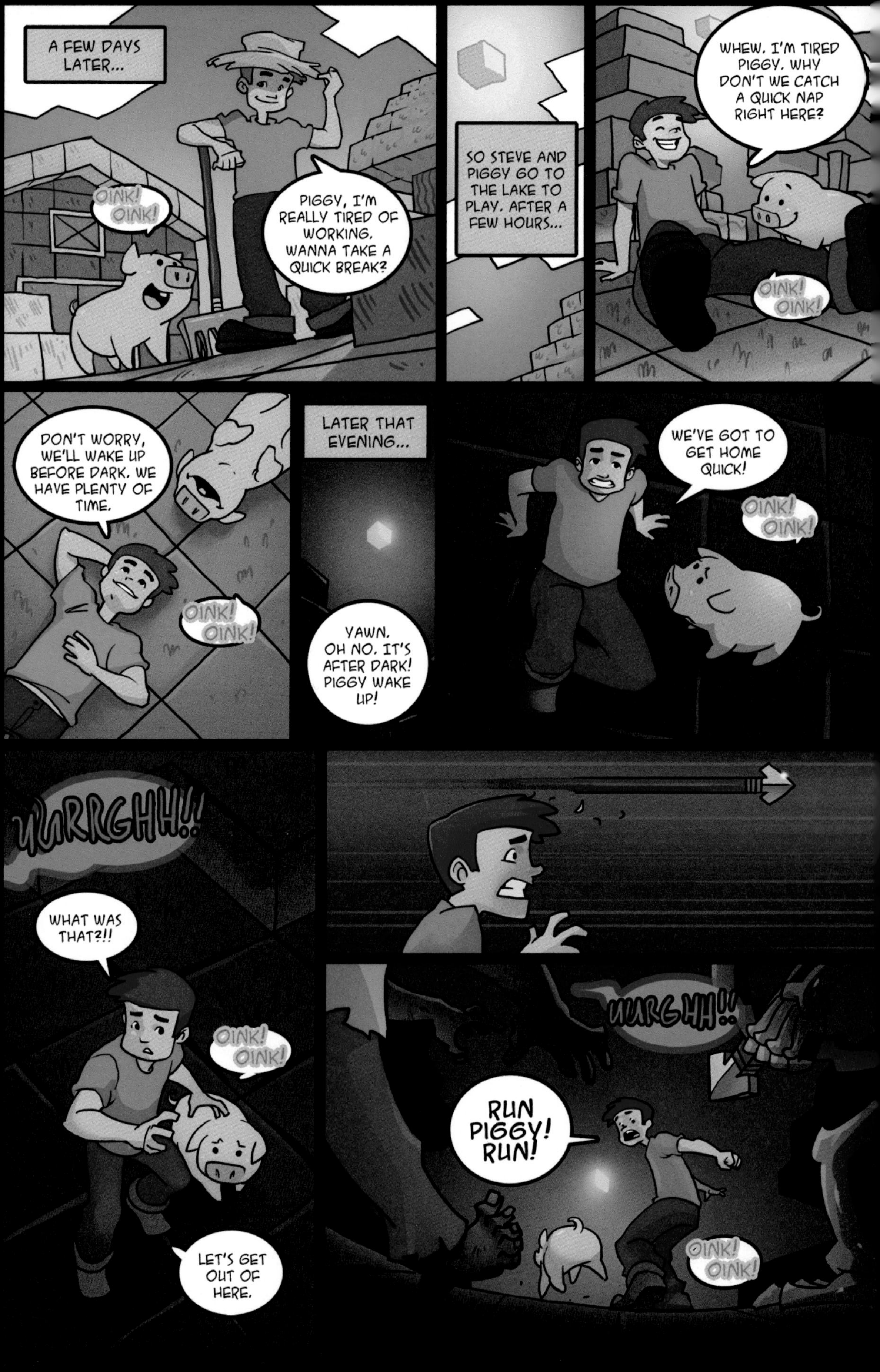
A FEW DAYS LATER...
OINK! OINK!
PIGGY, I'M REALLY TIRED OF WORKING. WANNA TAKE A QUICK BREAK?
SO STEVE AND PIGGY GO TO THE LAKE TO PLAY. AFTER A FEW HOURS...
WHEW. I'M TIRED PIGGY. WHY DON'T WE CATCH A QUICK NAP RIGHT HERE?
OINK! OINK!
DON'T WORRY, WE'LL WAKE UP BEFORE DARK. WE HAVE PLENTY OF TIME.
OINK! OINK!
LATER THAT EVENING...
YAWN. OH NO. IT'S AFTER DARK! PIGGY WAKE UP!
WE'VE GOT TO GET HOME QUICK!
OINK! OINK!
UURRGHH!!
WHAT WAS THAT?!!
OINK! OINK!
LET'S GET OUT OF HERE.
UURGHH!!
RUN PIGGY! RUN!
OINK! OINK!

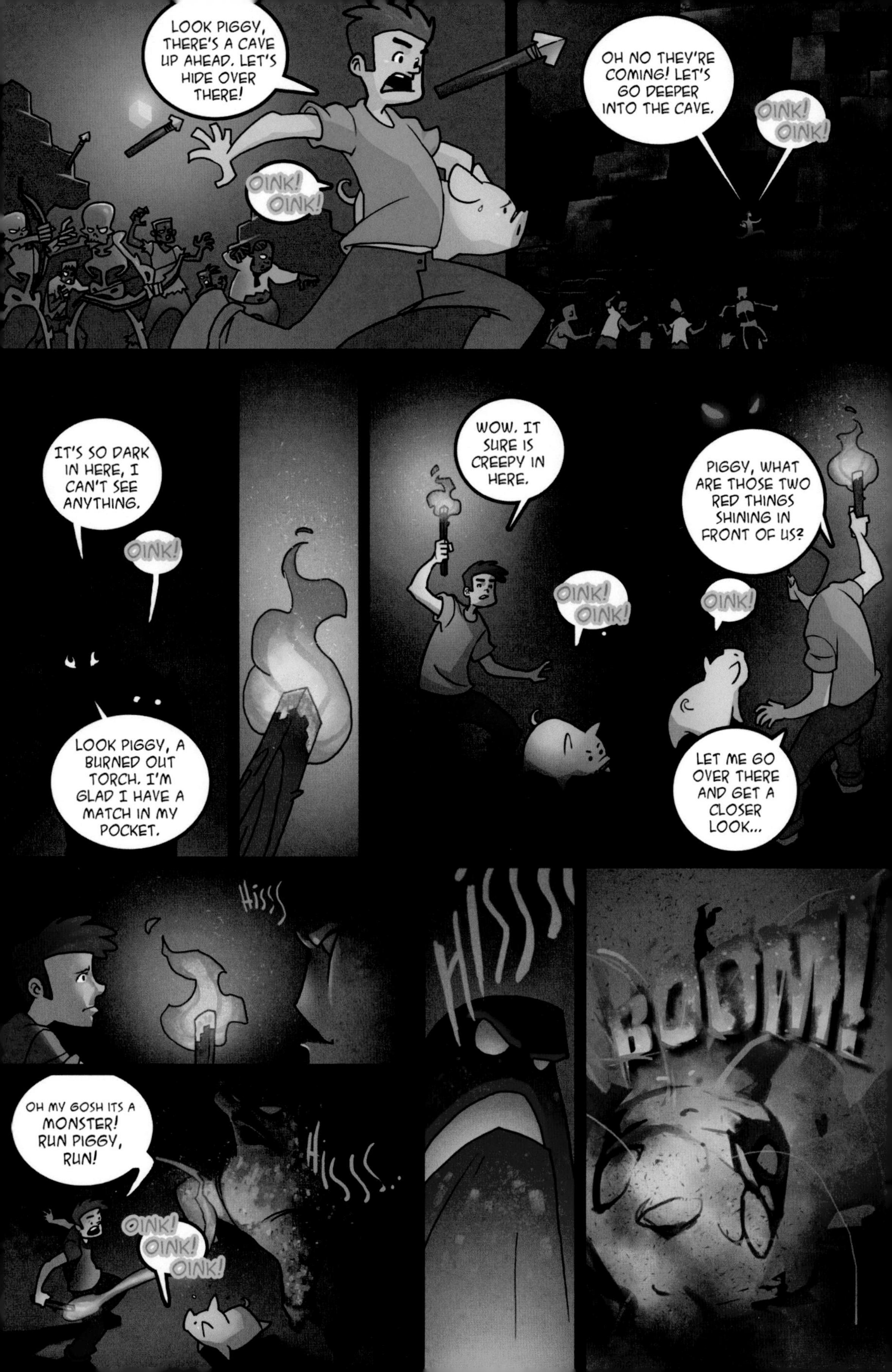
LOOK PIGGY, THERE'S A CAVE UP AHEAD. LET'S HIDE OVER THERE!
OINK! OINK!
OH NO THEY'RE COMING! LET'S GO DEEPER INTO THE CAVE.
OINK! OINK!
IT'S SO DARK IN HERE, I CAN'T SEE ANYTHING.
OINK!
LOOK PIGGY, A BURNED OUT TORCH. I'M GLAD I HAVE A MATCH IN MY POCKET.
WOW. IT SURE IS CREEPY IN HERE.
OINK! OINK!
PIGGY, WHAT ARE THOSE TWO RED THINGS SHINING IN FRONT OF US?
OINK!
LET ME GO OVER THERE AND GET A CLOSER LOOK...
HISSS
OH MY GOSH ITS A MONSTER! RUN PIGGY, RUN!
HISSS...
OINK! OINK! OINK!
HISSS
BOOM!

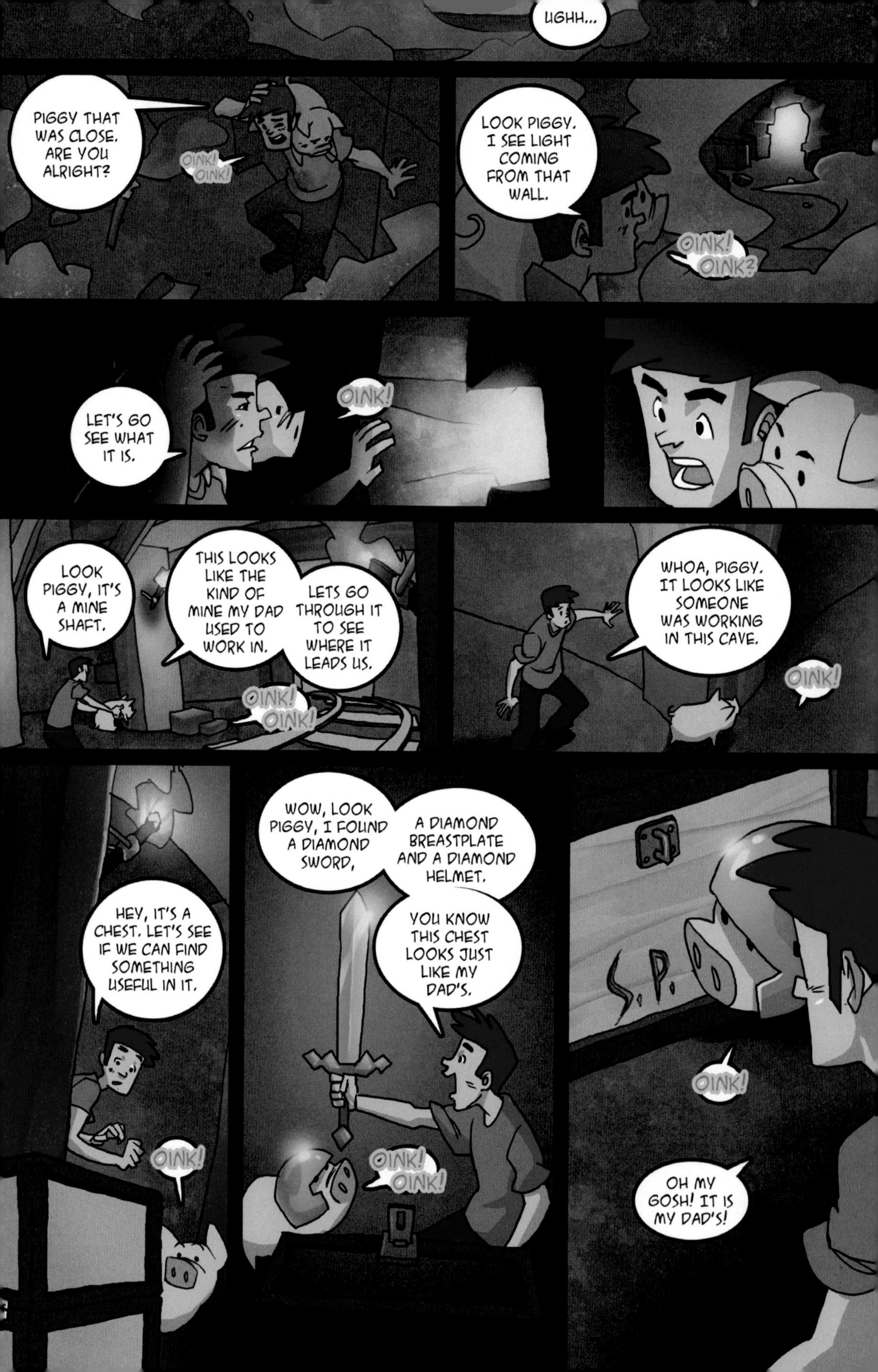
UGHH...
PIGGY THAT WAS CLOSE. ARE YOU ALRIGHT?
OINK! OINK!
LOOK PIGGY. I SEE LIGHT COMING FROM THAT WALL.
OINK! OINK?
LET'S GO SEE WHAT IT IS.
OINK!
LOOK PIGGY, IT'S A MINE SHAFT.
THIS LOOKS LIKE THE KIND OF MINE MY DAD USED TO WORK IN.
LETS GO THROUGH IT TO SEE WHERE IT LEADS US.
OINK! OINK!
WHOA, PIGGY. IT LOOKS LIKE SOMEONE WAS WORKING IN THIS CAVE.
OINK!
HEY, IT'S A CHEST. LET'S SEE IF WE CAN FIND SOMETHING USEFUL IN IT.
OINK!
WOW, LOOK PIGGY, I FOUND A DIAMOND SWORD,
A DIAMOND BREASTPLATE AND A DIAMOND HELMET.
YOU KNOW THIS CHEST LOOKS JUST LIKE MY DAD'S.
OINK! OINK!
S. P.
OINK!
OH MY GOSH! IT IS MY DAD'S!

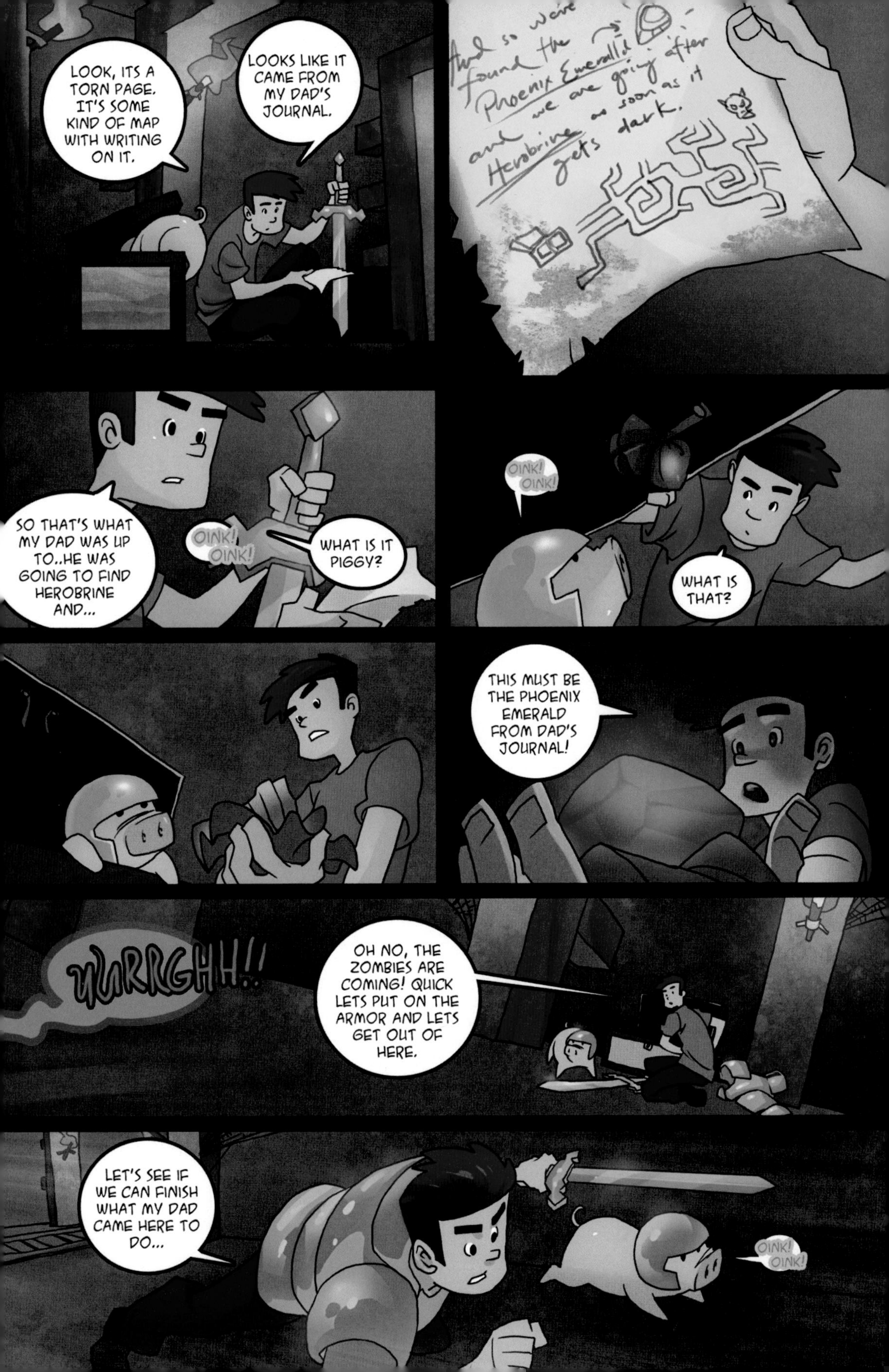

LOOK, ITS A TORN PAGE. IT'S SOME KIND OF MAP WITH WRITING ON IT.
LOOKS LIKE IT CAME FROM MY DAD'S JOURNAL.
And so we've found the Phoenix Emerald
and we are going after Herobrine as soon as it gets dark.
SO THAT'S WHAT MY DAD WAS UP TO..HE WAS GOING TO FIND HEROBRINE AND...
OINK! OINK!
WHAT IS IT PIGGY?
OINK! OINK!
WHAT IS THAT?
THIS MUST BE THE PHOENIX EMERALD FROM DAD'S JOURNAL!
UURRGHH!!
OH NO, THE ZOMBIES ARE COMING! QUICK LETS PUT ON THE ARMOR AND LETS GET OUT OF HERE.
LET'S SEE IF WE CAN FINISH WHAT MY DAD CAME HERE TO DO...
OINK! OINK!

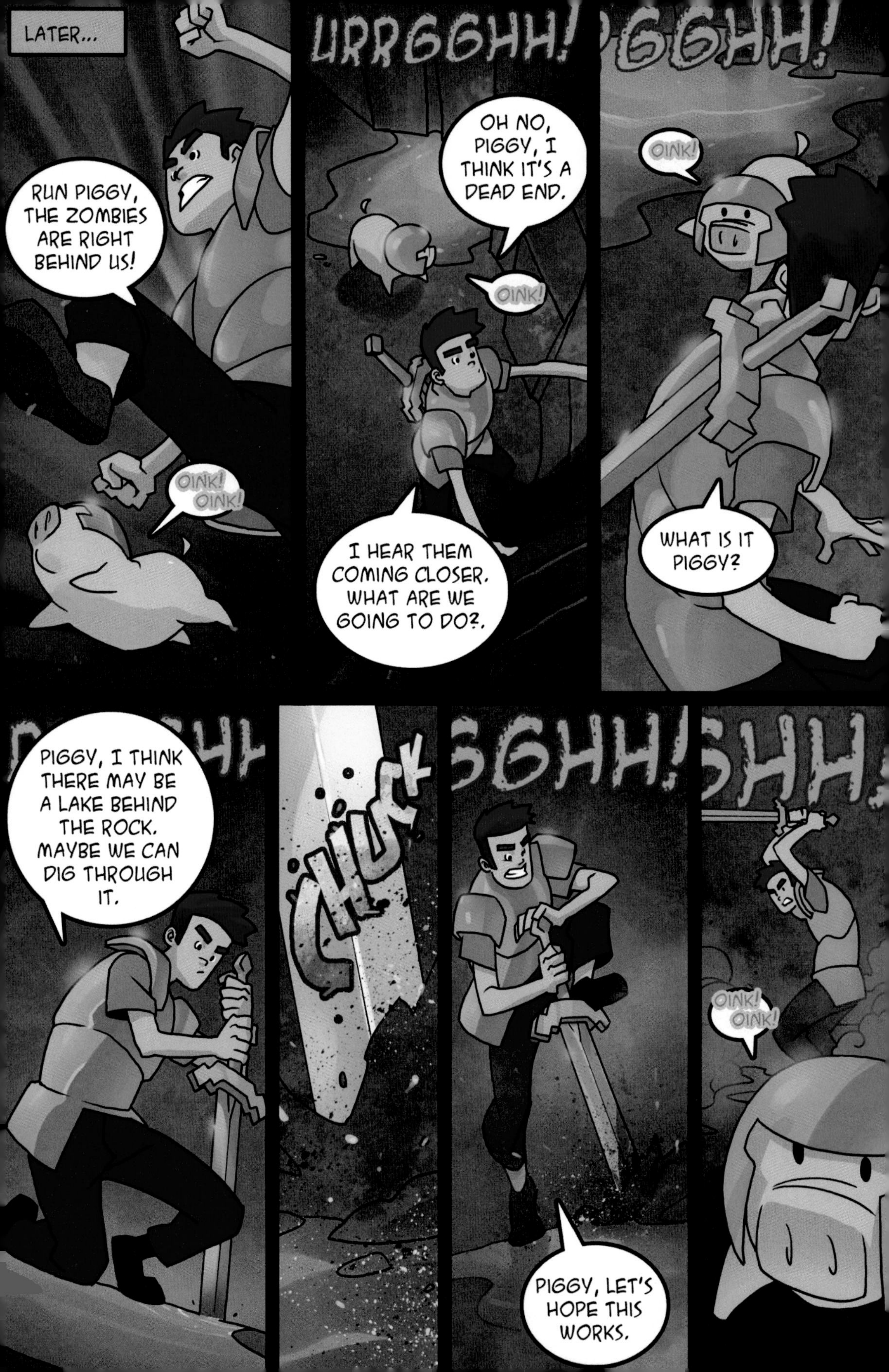
LATER...
RUN PIGGY, THE ZOMBIES ARE RIGHT BEHIND US!
OINK! OINK!
URRGGHH!
OH NO, PIGGY, I THINK IT'S A DEAD END.
OINK!
I HEAR THEM COMING CLOSER. WHAT ARE WE GOING TO DO?
GGHH!
OINK!
WHAT IS IT PIGGY?
PIGGY, I THINK THERE MAY BE A LAKE BEHIND THE ROCK. MAYBE WE CAN DIG THROUGH IT.
CHUCK
GGHH!
PIGGY, LET'S HOPE THIS WORKS.
GHH!
OINK! OINK!

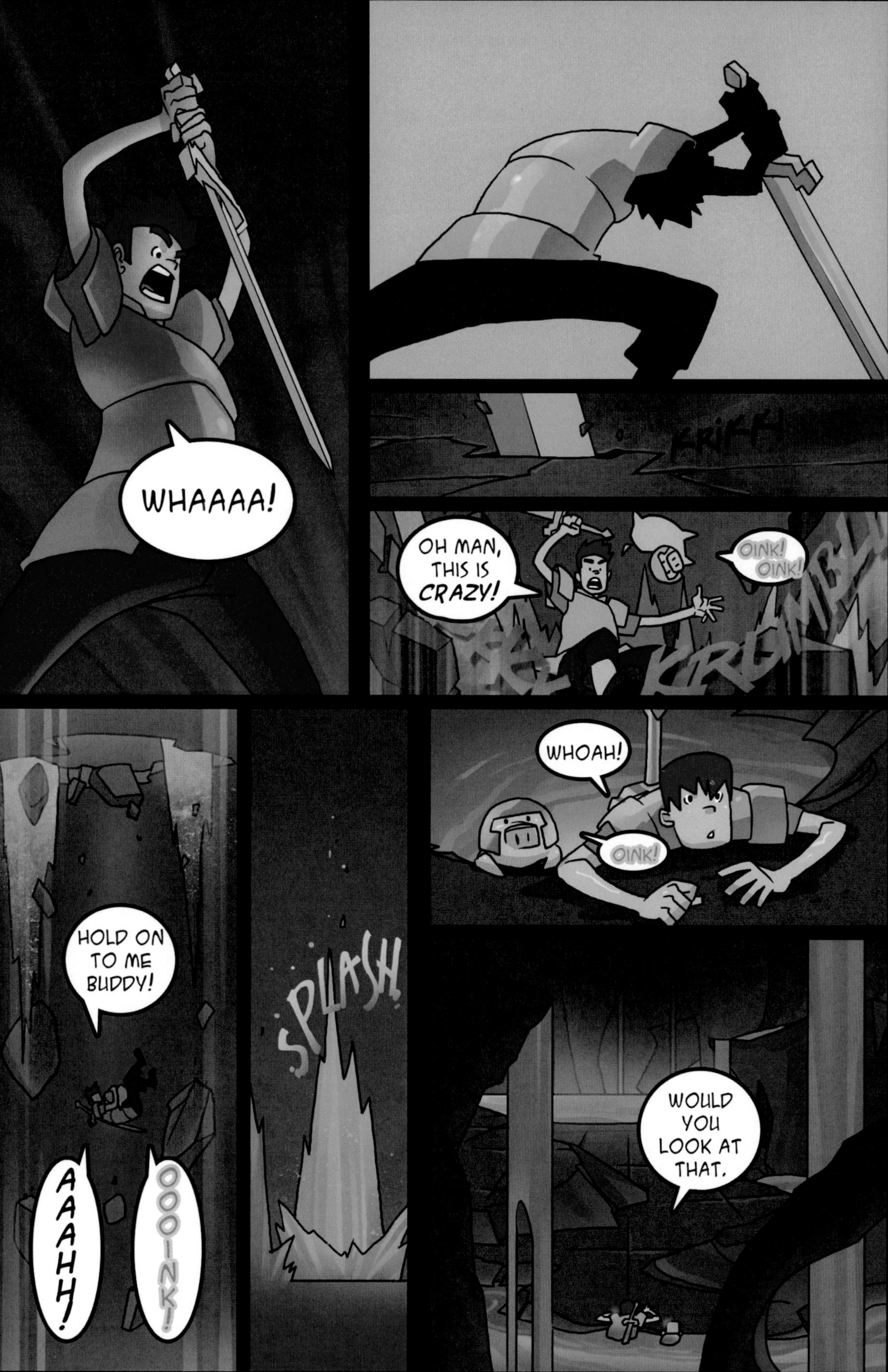
WHAAAA!
KRIKK!
OH MAN, THIS IS CRAZY!
OINK! OINK!
KRUMBL
WHOAH!
OINK!
HOLD ON TO ME BUDDY!
AAAHH!
OOOINK!
SPLASH!
WOULD YOU LOOK AT THAT.

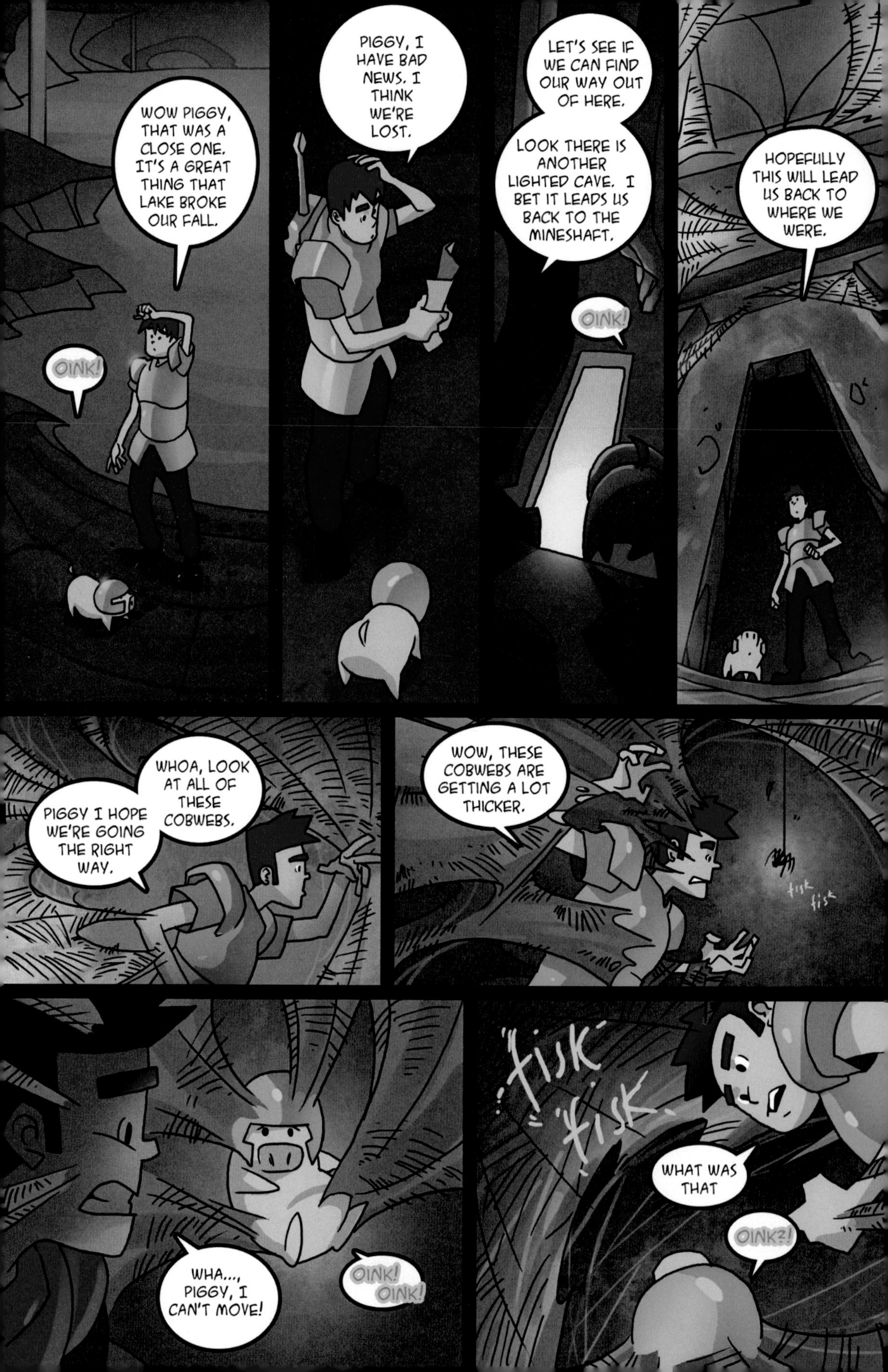
WOW PIGGY, THAT WAS A CLOSE ONE. IT'S A GREAT THING THAT LAKE BROKE OUR FALL.
OINK!
PIGGY, I HAVE BAD NEWS. I THINK WE'RE LOST.
LET'S SEE IF WE CAN FIND OUR WAY OUT OF HERE.
LOOK THERE IS ANOTHER LIGHTED CAVE. I BET IT LEADS US BACK TO THE MINESHAFT.
OINK!
HOPEFULLY THIS WILL LEAD US BACK TO WHERE WE WERE.
WHOA, LOOK AT ALL OF THESE COBWEBS.
PIGGY I HOPE WE'RE GOING THE RIGHT WAY.
WOW, THESE COBWEBS ARE GETTING A LOT THICKER.
fisk fisk
WHA..., PIGGY, I CAN'T MOVE!
OINK! OINK!
fisk fisk
WHAT WAS THAT
OINK?!

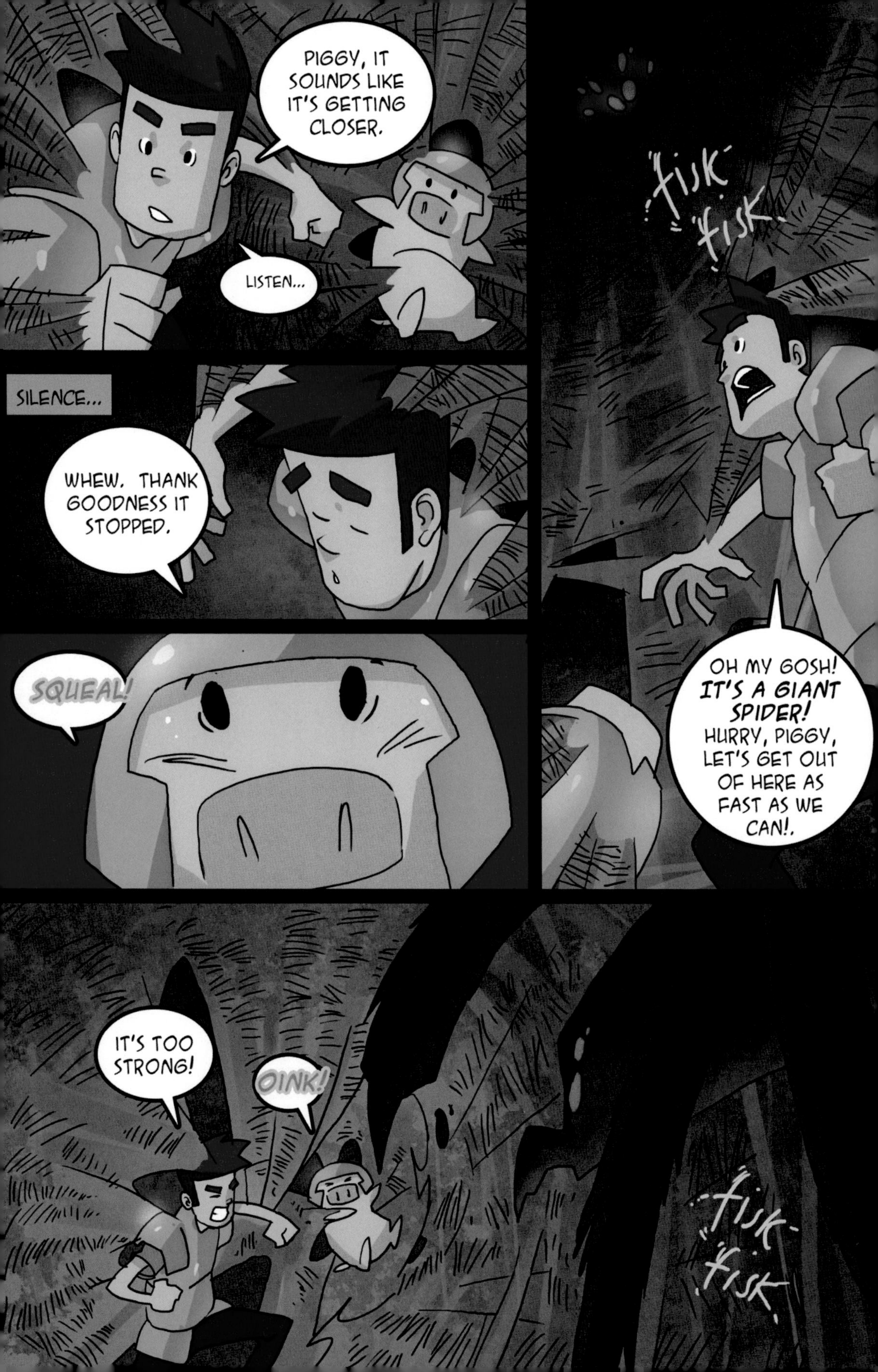
PIGGY, IT SOUNDS LIKE IT'S GETTING CLOSER.
LISTEN...
TISK TISK
SILENCE...
WHEW. THANK GOODNESS IT STOPPED.
SQUEAL!
OH MY GOSH! IT'S A GIANT SPIDER! HURRY, PIGGY, LET'S GET OUT OF HERE AS FAST AS WE CAN!.
IT'S TOO STRONG!
OINK!
TISK TISK

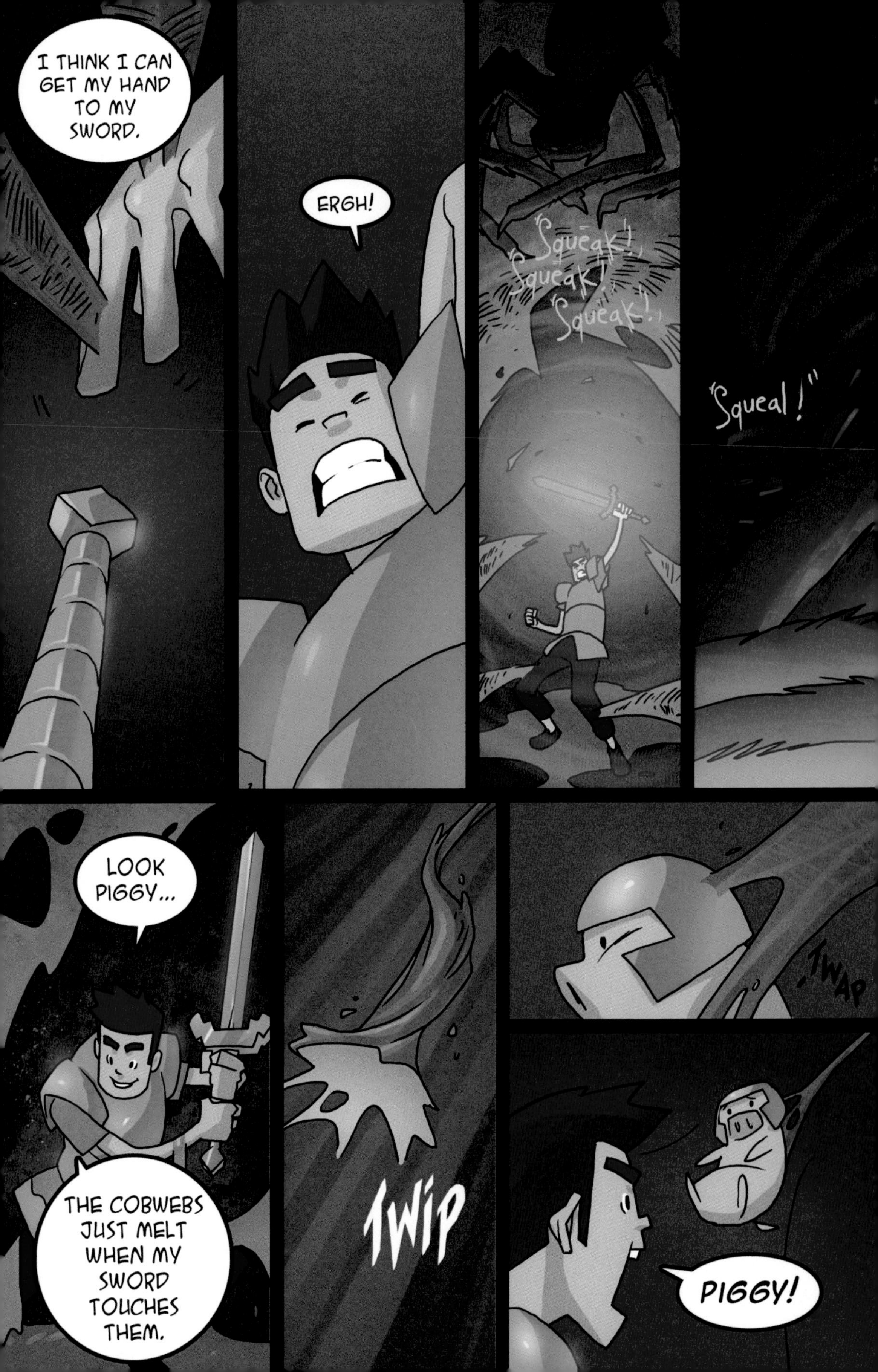
I THINK I CAN GET MY HAND TO MY SWORD.
ERGH!
"Squeak!" "Squeak!" "Squeak!"
"Squeal!"
LOOK PIGGY...
THE COBWEBS JUST MELT WHEN MY SWORD TOUCHES THEM.
TWIP
TWAP
PIGGY!

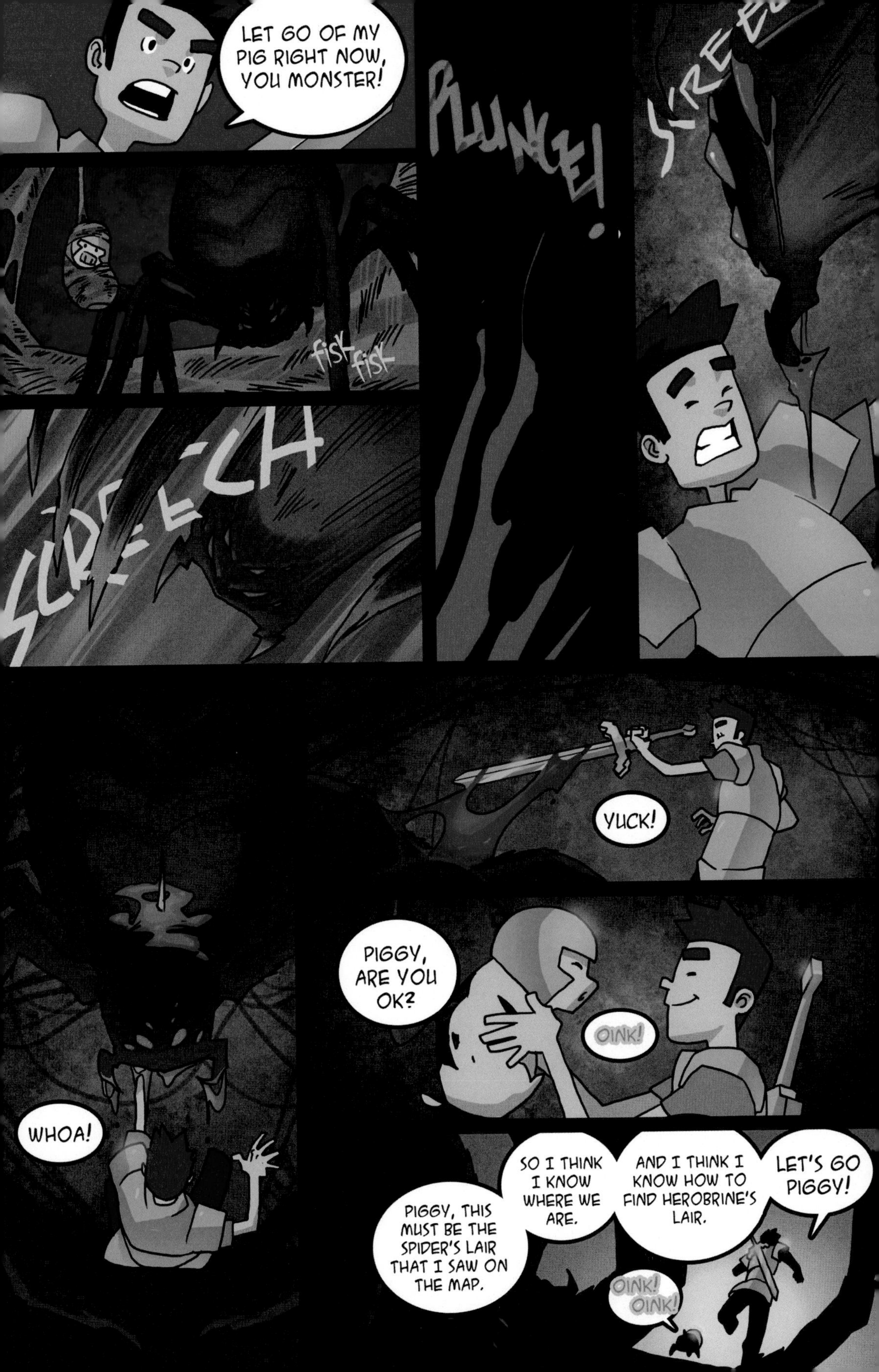

LET GO OF MY PIG RIGHT NOW, YOU MONSTER!
fisk fisk
SCREECH
PLUNGE!
SCREE
YUCK!
WHOA!
PIGGY, ARE YOU OK?
OINK!
PIGGY, THIS MUST BE THE SPIDER'S LAIR THAT I SAW ON THE MAP.
SO I THINK I KNOW WHERE WE ARE.
AND I THINK I KNOW HOW TO FIND HEROBRINE'S LAIR.
LET'S GO PIGGY!
OINK! OINK!

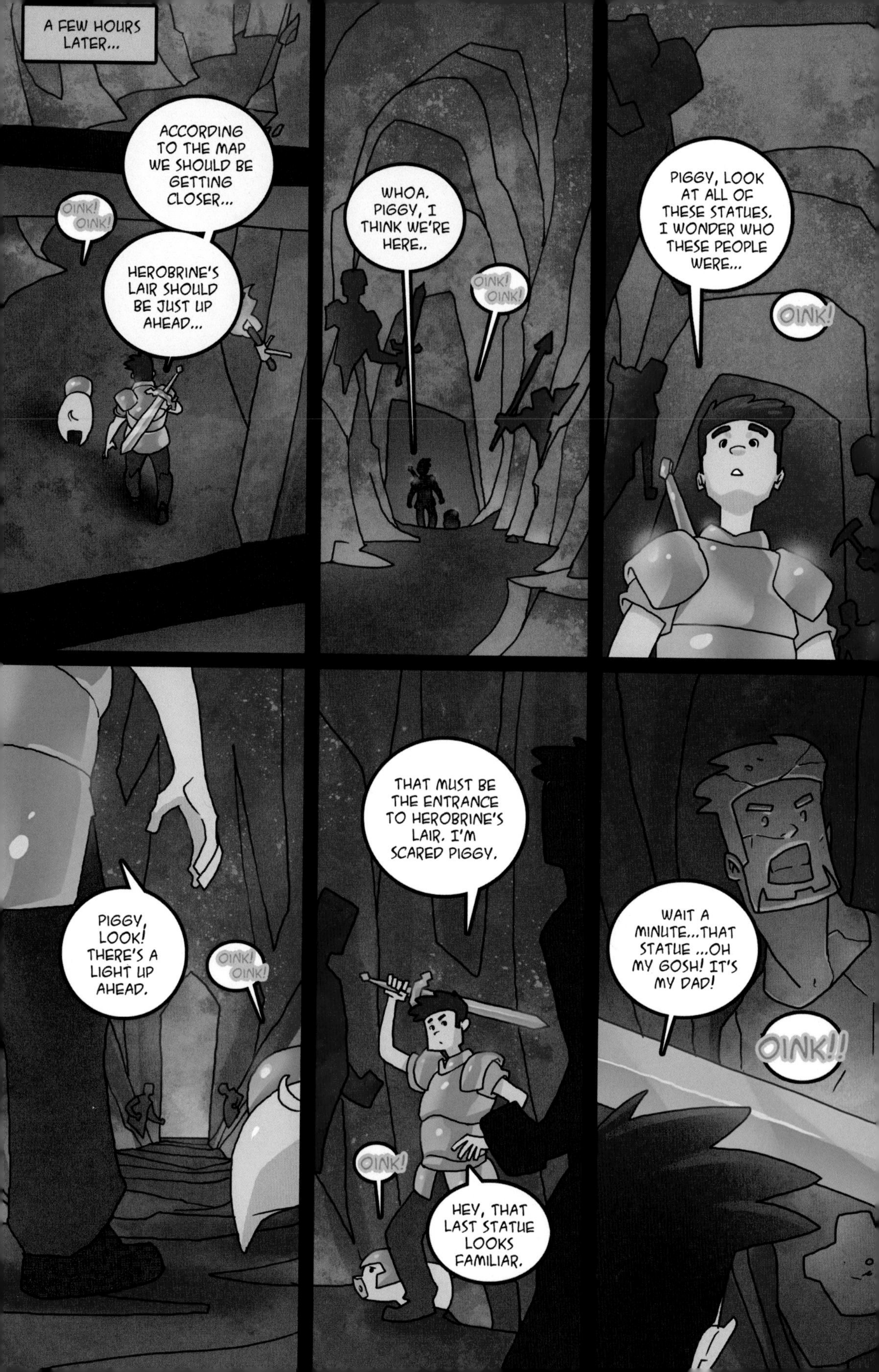
A FEW HOURS LATER...
ACCORDING TO THE MAP WE SHOULD BE GETTING CLOSER...
OINK! OINK!
HEROBRINE'S LAIR SHOULD BE JUST UP AHEAD...
WHOA. PIGGY, I THINK WE'RE HERE..
OINK! OINK!
PIGGY, LOOK AT ALL OF THESE STATUES. I WONDER WHO THESE PEOPLE WERE...
OINK!
PIGGY, LOOK! THERE'S A LIGHT UP AHEAD.
OINK! OINK!
THAT MUST BE THE ENTRANCE TO HEROBRINE'S LAIR. I'M SCARED PIGGY.
OINK!
HEY, THAT LAST STATUE LOOKS FAMILIAR.
WAIT A MINUTE...THAT STATUE ...OH MY GOSH! IT'S MY DAD!
OINK!!

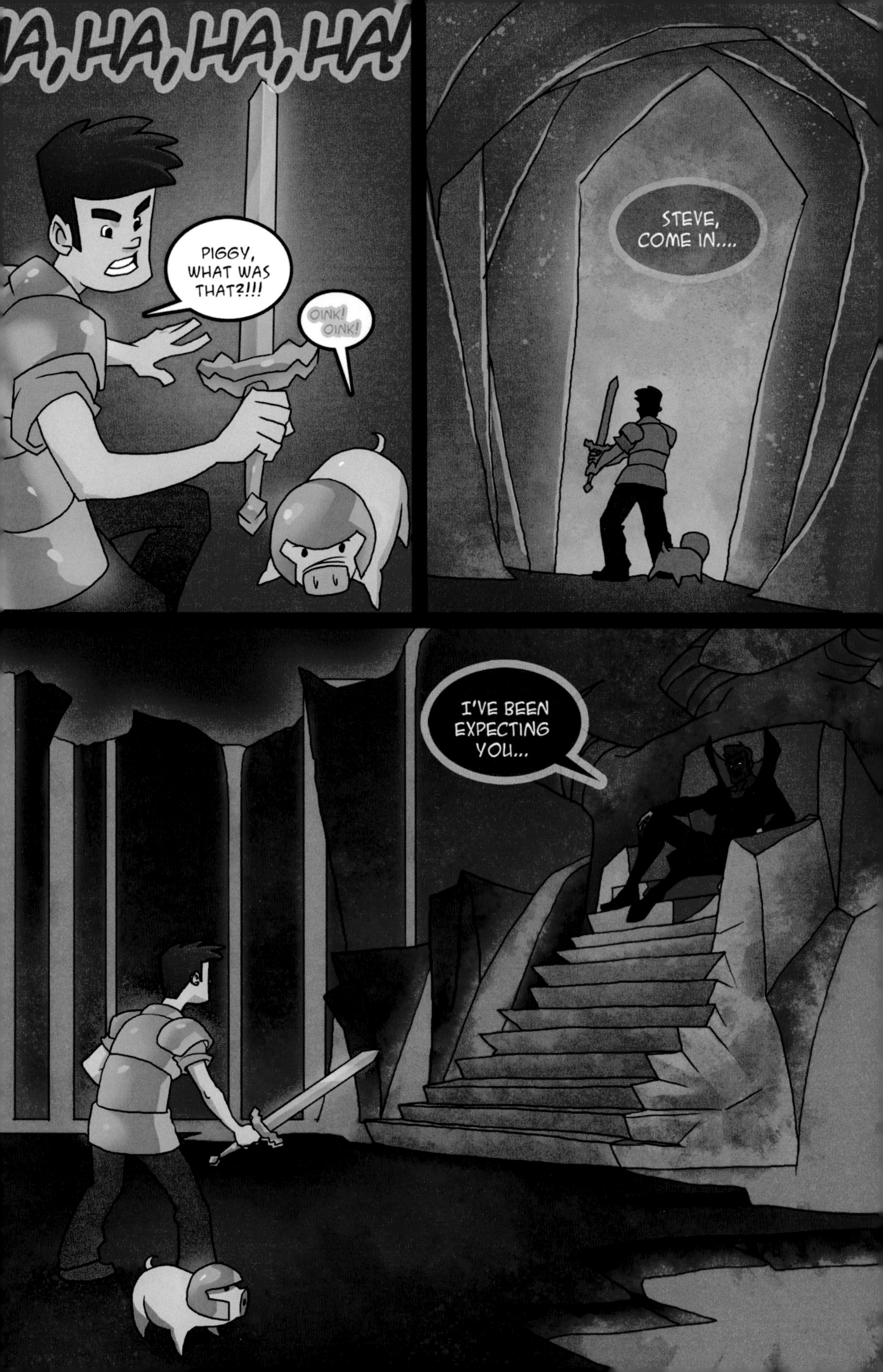
HA, HA, HA, HA!
PIGGY, WHAT WAS THAT?!!!
OINK! OINK!
STEVE, COME IN....
I'VE BEEN EXPECTING YOU...

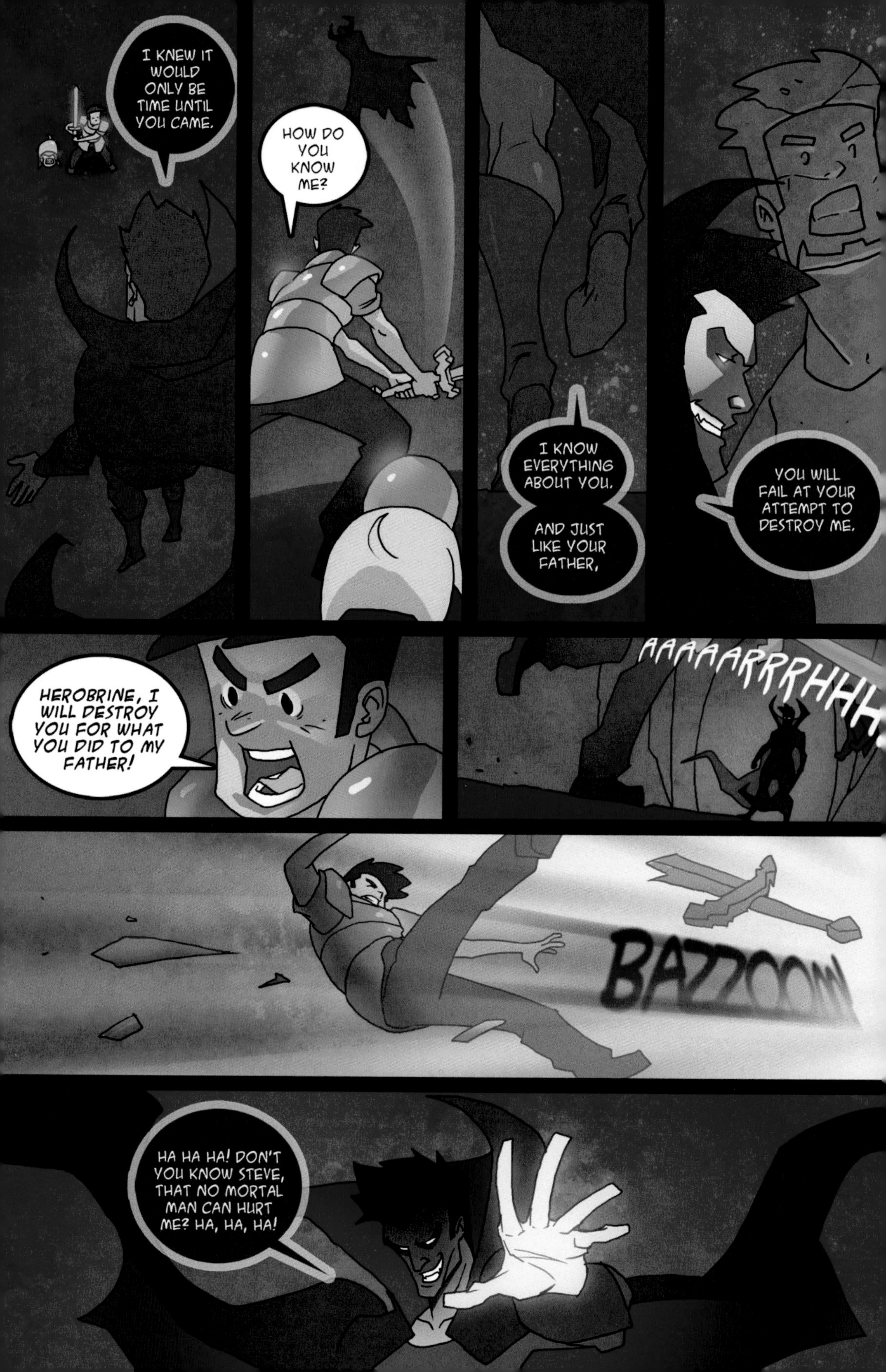
I KNEW IT WOULD ONLY BE TIME UNTIL YOU CAME.
HOW DO YOU KNOW ME?
I KNOW EVERYTHING ABOUT YOU.
AND JUST LIKE YOUR FATHER,
YOU WILL FAIL AT YOUR ATTEMPT TO DESTROY ME.
HEROBRINE, I WILL DESTROY YOU FOR WHAT YOU DID TO MY FATHER!
AAAAARRRHHH
BAZZOOM
HA HA HA! DON'T YOU KNOW STEVE, THAT NO MORTAL MAN CAN HURT ME? HA, HA, HA!

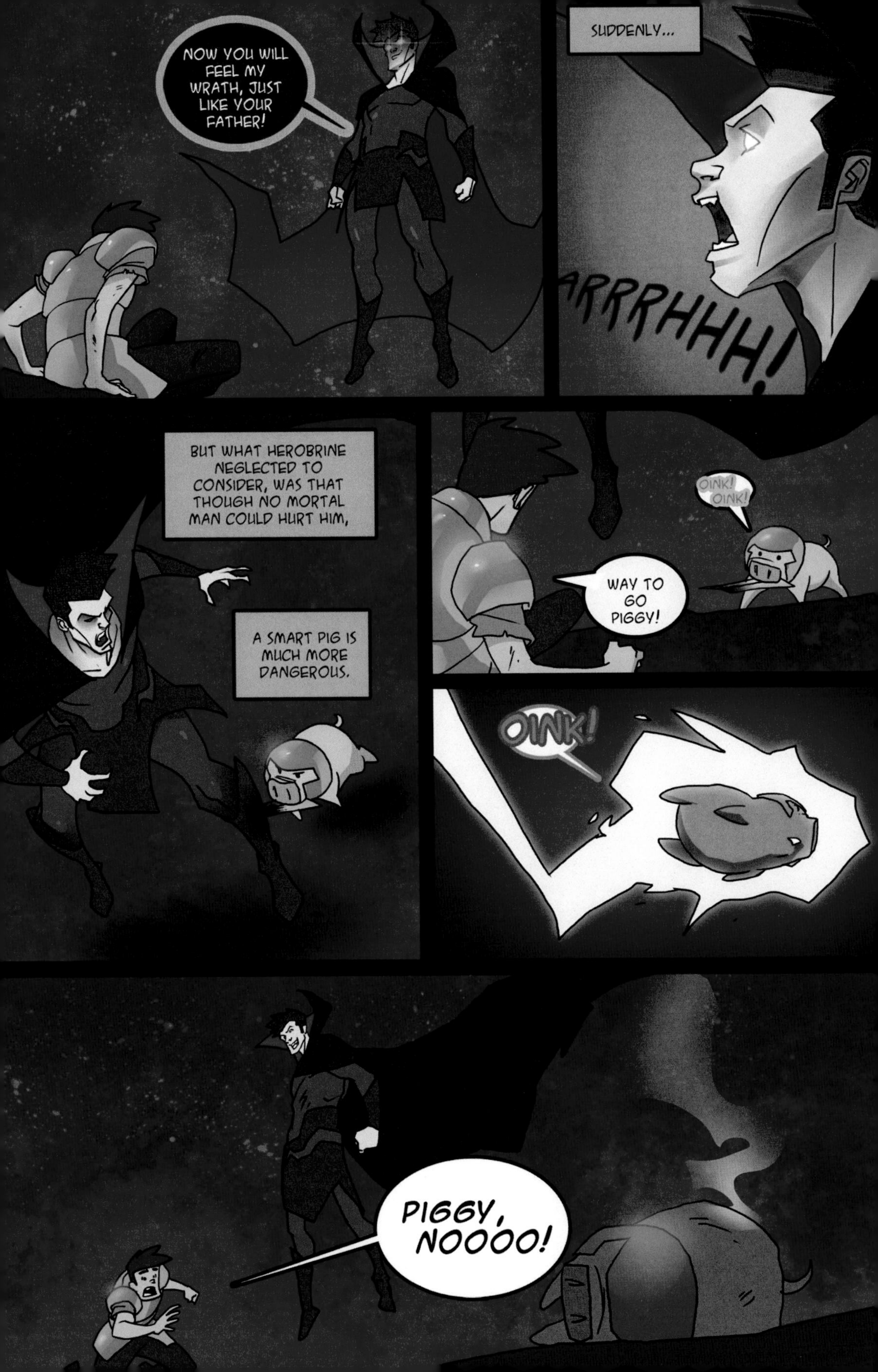
NOW YOU WILL FEEL MY WRATH, JUST LIKE YOUR FATHER!
SUDDENLY...
ARRRHHH!
BUT WHAT HEROBRINE NEGLECTED TO CONSIDER, WAS THAT THOUGH NO MORTAL MAN COULD HURT HIM,
A SMART PIG IS MUCH MORE DANGEROUS.
OINK! OINK!
WAY TO GO PIGGY!
OINK!
PIGGY, NOOOO!

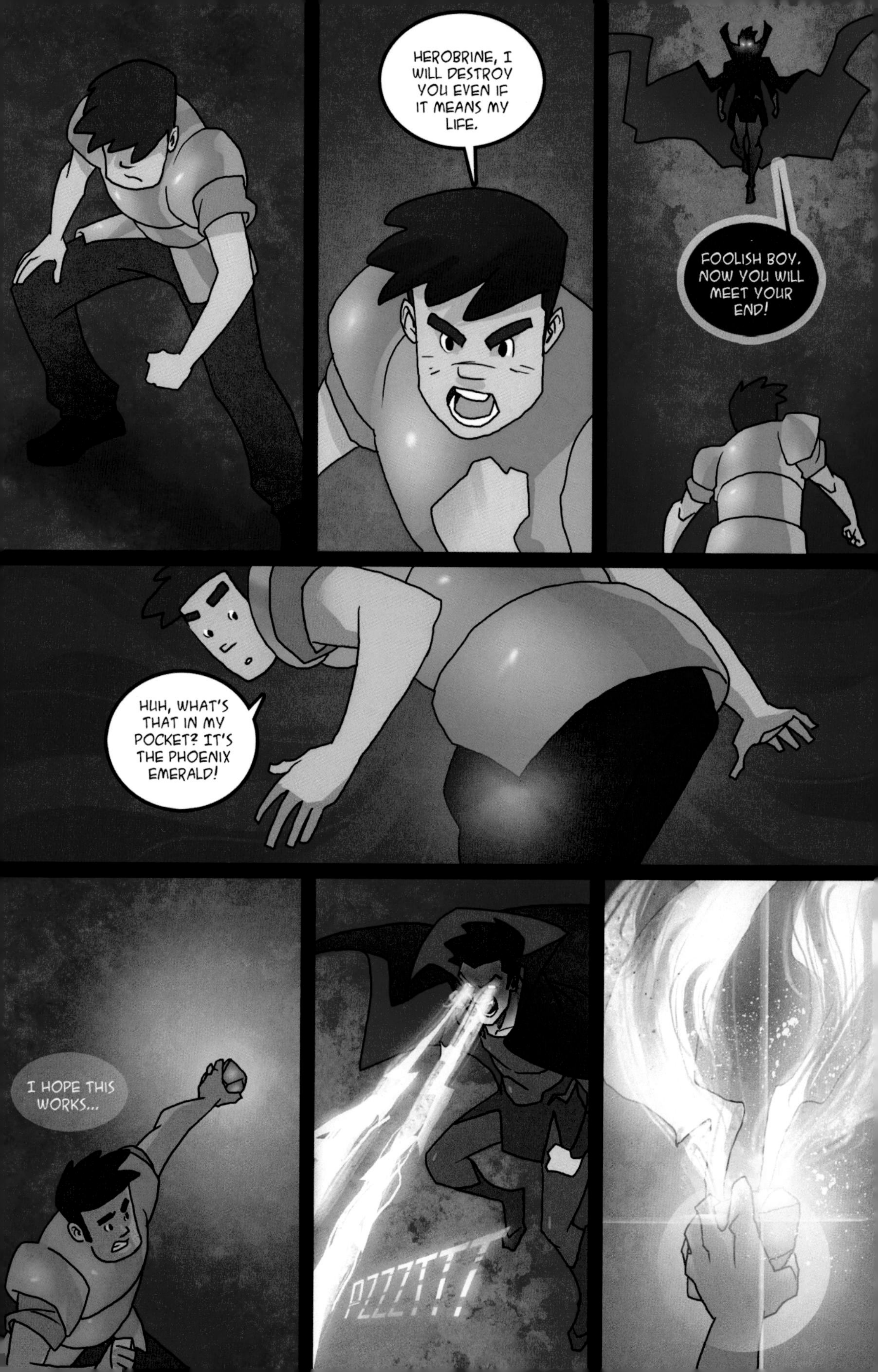
HEROBRINE, I WILL DESTROY YOU EVEN IF IT MEANS MY LIFE.
FOOLISH BOY. NOW YOU WILL MEET YOUR END!
HUH, WHAT'S THAT IN MY POCKET? IT'S THE PHOENIX EMERALD!
I HOPE THIS WORKS...
PZZZTTT!

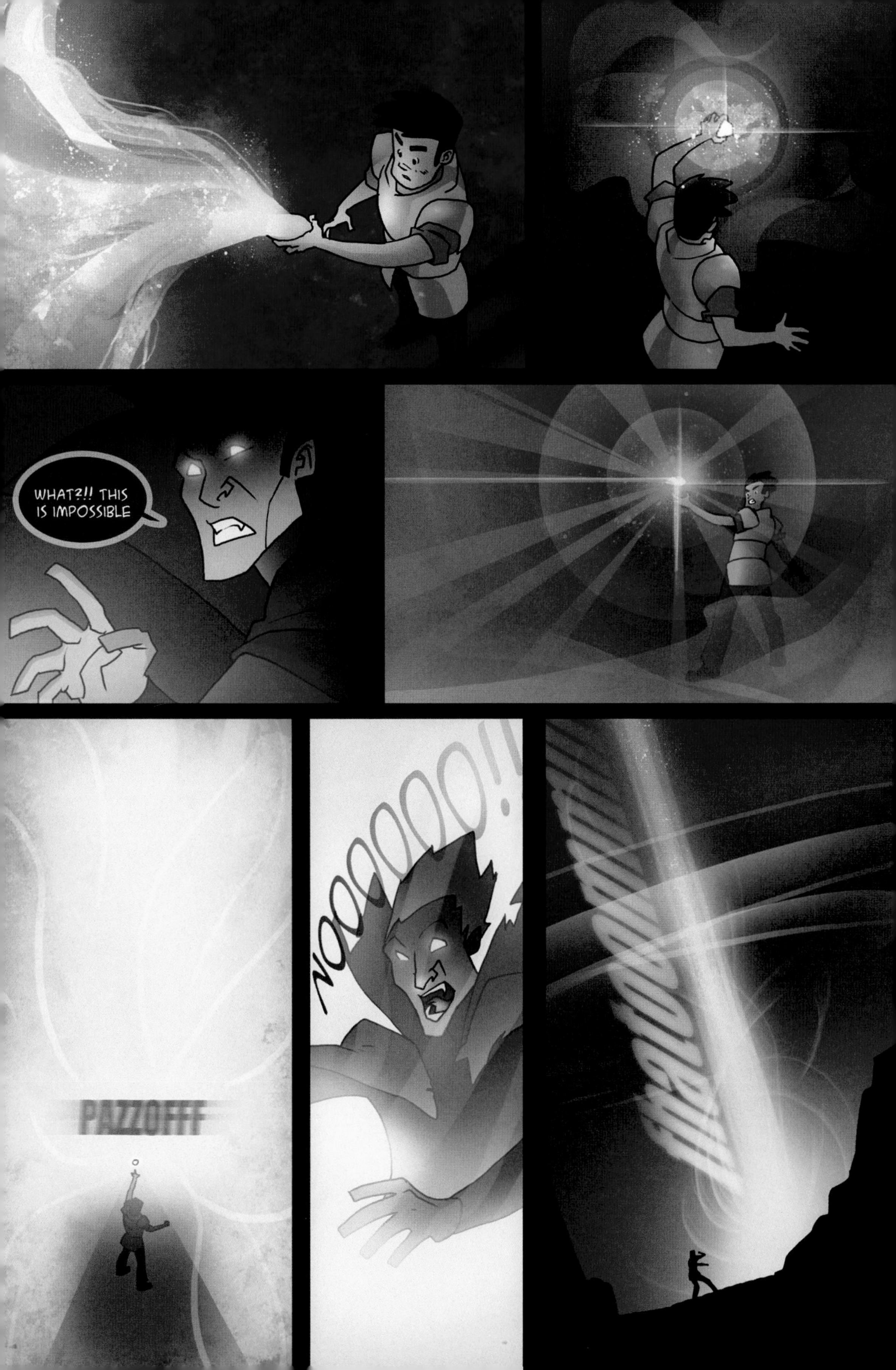
WHAT?!! THIS IS IMPOSSIBLE
PAZZOFFF
NOOOOOOO!!

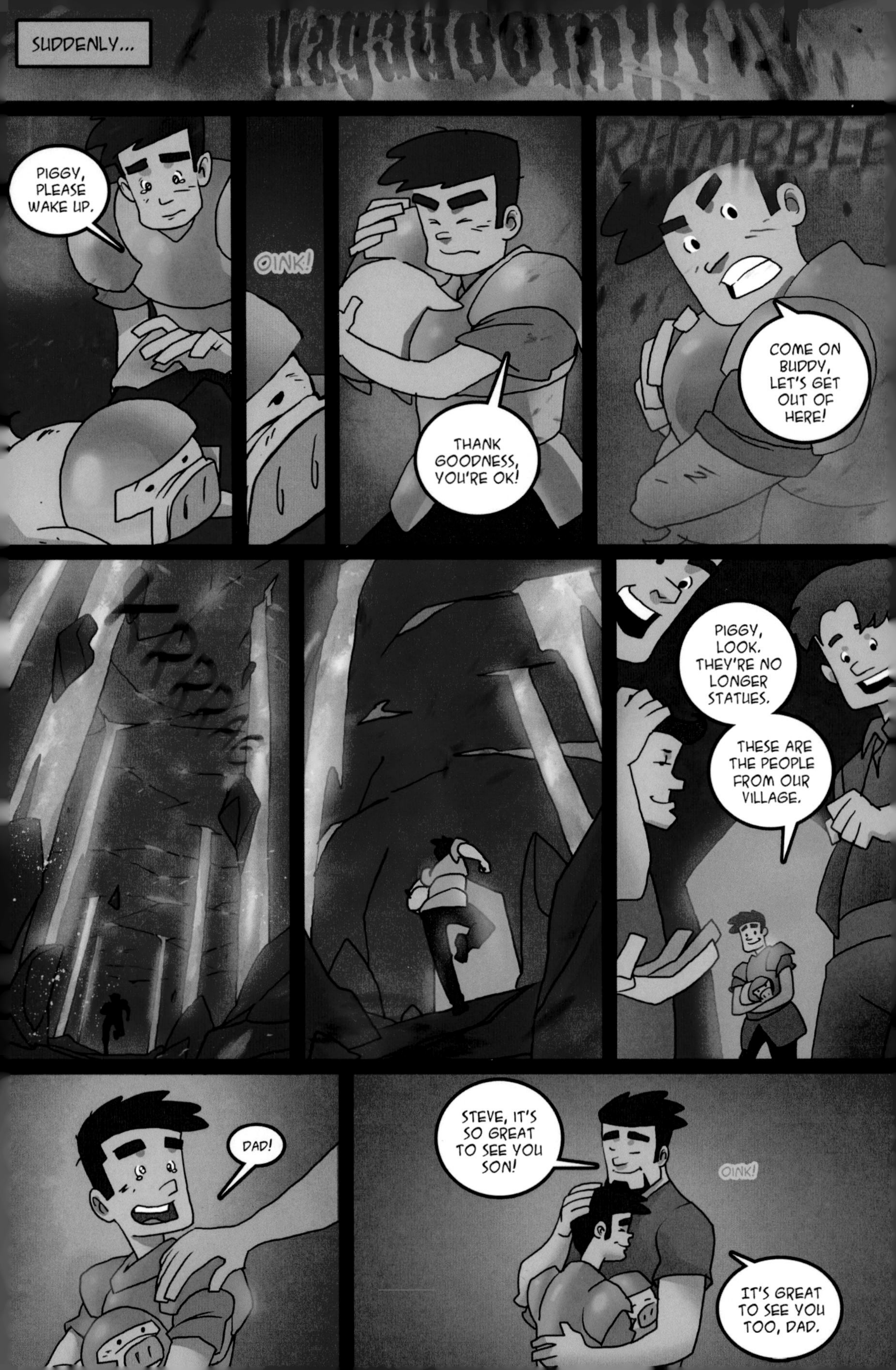
SUDDENLY...
PIGGY, PLEASE WAKE UP.
OINK!
THANK GOODNESS, YOU'RE OK!
COME ON BUDDY, LET'S GET OUT OF HERE!
PIGGY, LOOK. THEY'RE NO LONGER STATUES.
THESE ARE THE PEOPLE FROM OUR VILLAGE.
DAD!
STEVE, IT'S SO GREAT TO SEE YOU SON!
OINK!
IT'S GREAT TO SEE YOU TOO, DAD.

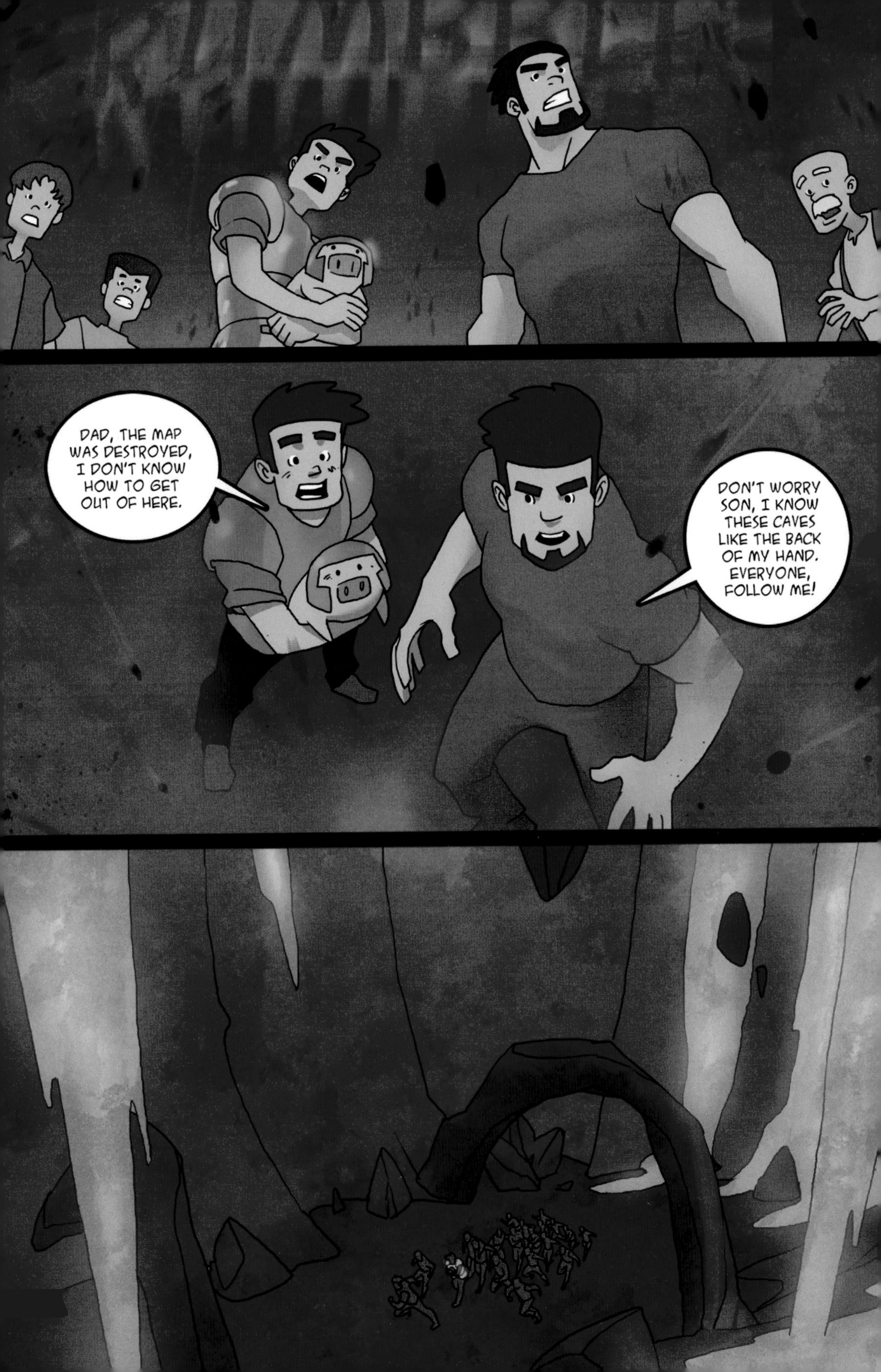
DAD, THE MAP WAS DESTROYED, I DON'T KNOW HOW TO GET OUT OF HERE.
DON'T WORRY SON, I KNOW THESE CAVES LIKE THE BACK OF MY HAND. EVERYONE, FOLLOW ME!

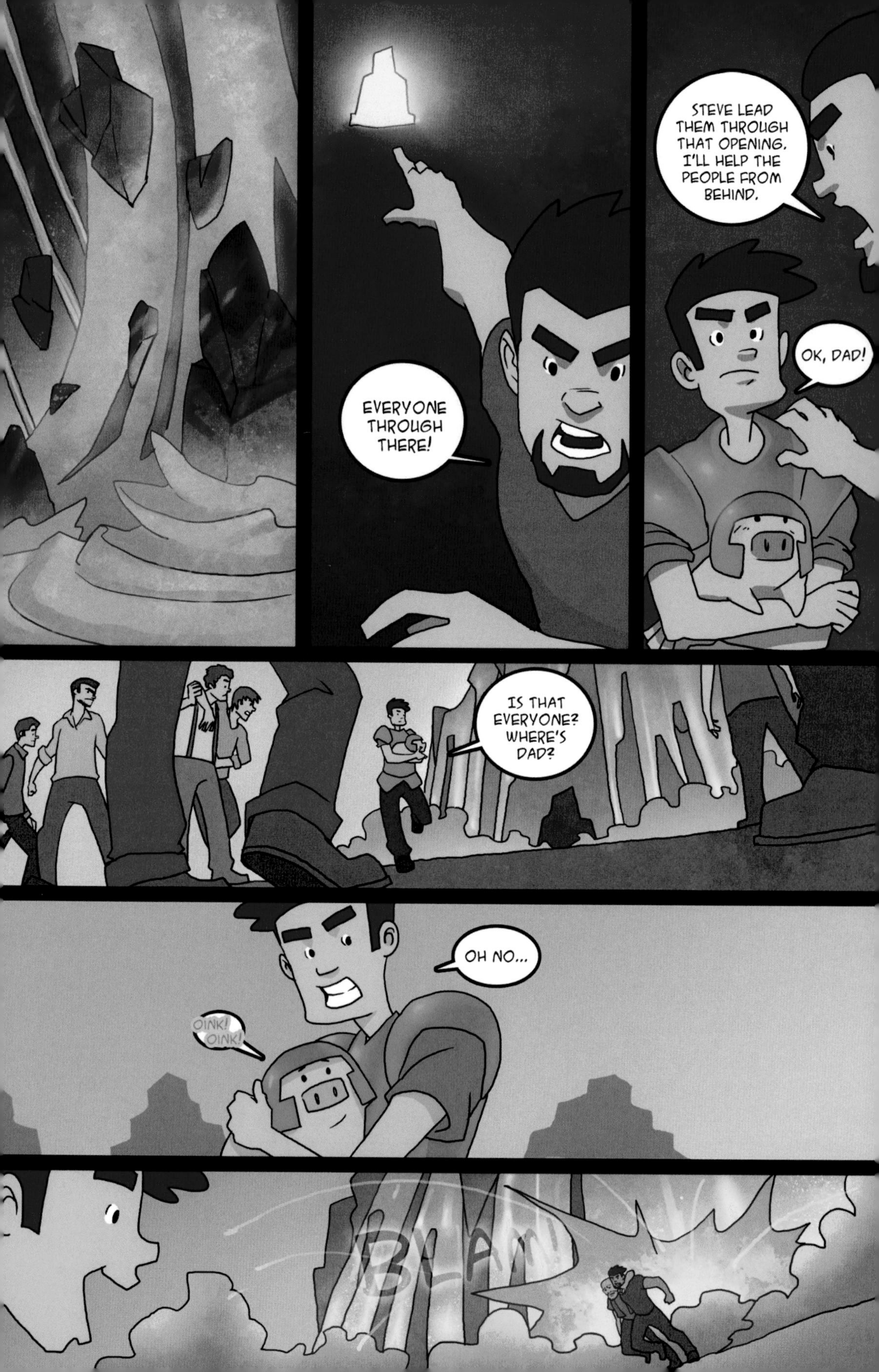
EVERYONE THROUGH THERE!
STEVE LEAD THEM THROUGH THAT OPENING. I'LL HELP THE PEOPLE FROM BEHIND.
OK, DAD!
IS THAT EVERYONE? WHERE'S DAD?
OH NO...
OINK! OINK!
BLAM!

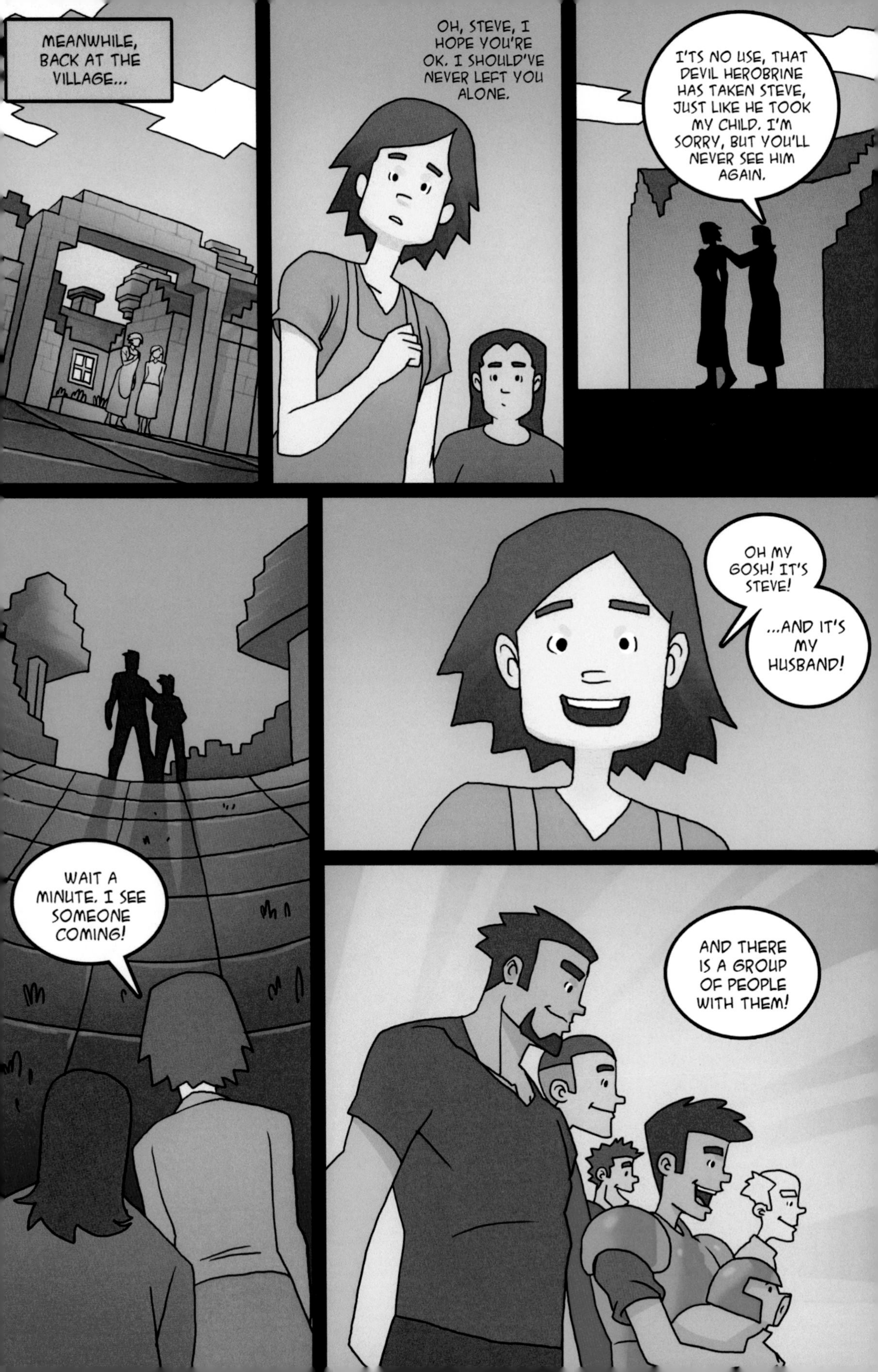
MEANWHILE, BACK AT THE VILLAGE...
OH, STEVE, I HOPE YOU'RE OK. I SHOULD'VE NEVER LEFT YOU ALONE.
I'TS NO USE, THAT DEVIL HEROBRINE HAS TAKEN STEVE, JUST LIKE HE TOOK MY CHILD. I'M SORRY, BUT YOU'LL NEVER SEE HIM AGAIN.
WAIT A MINUTE. I SEE SOMEONE COMING!
OH MY GOSH! IT'S STEVE!
...AND IT'S MY HUSBAND!
AND THERE IS A GROUP OF PEOPLE WITH THEM!

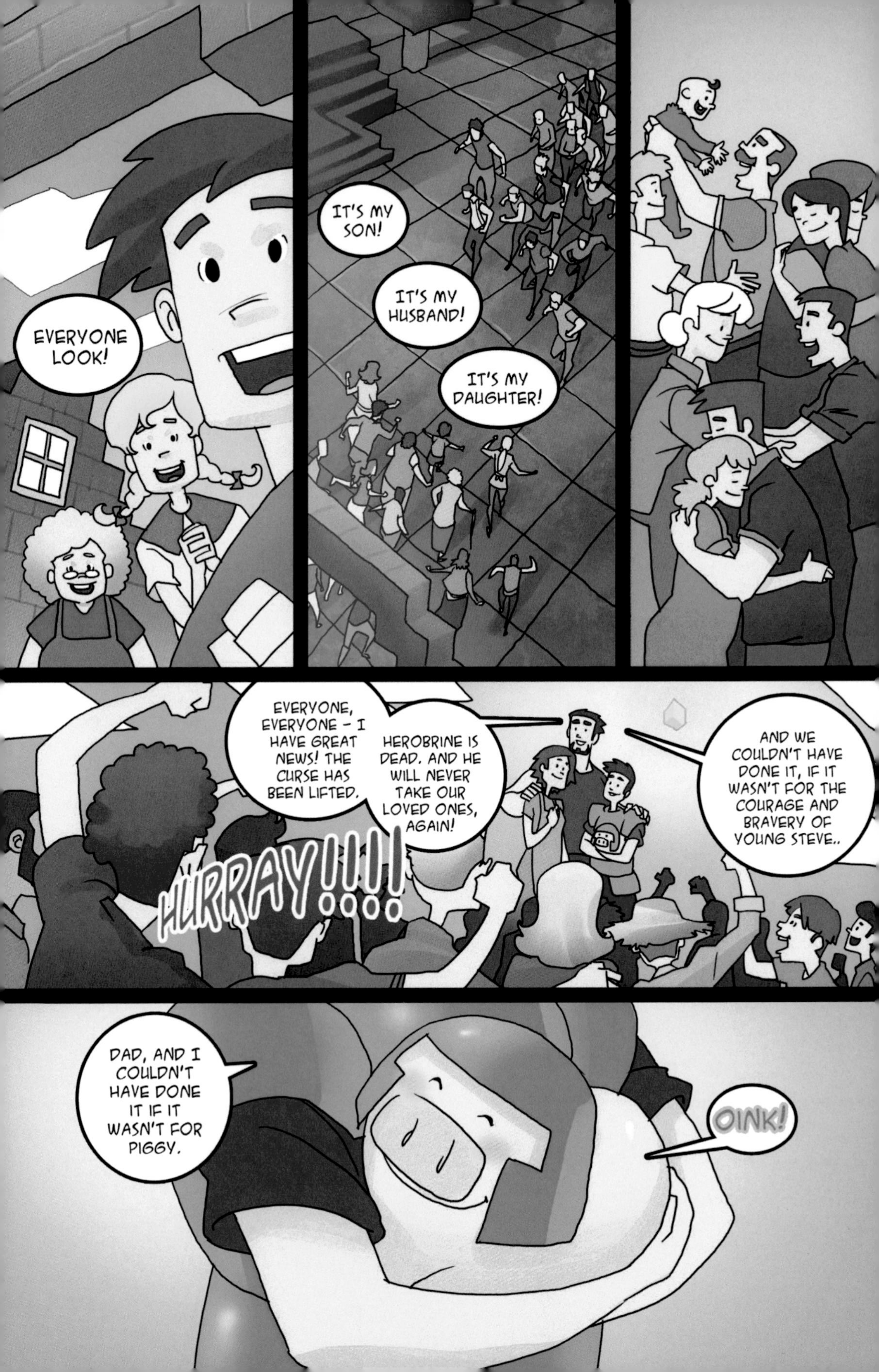
EVERYONE LOOK!
IT'S MY SON!
IT'S MY HUSBAND!
IT'S MY DAUGHTER!
EVERYONE, EVERYONE – I HAVE GREAT NEWS! THE CURSE HAS BEEN LIFTED.
HERORBRINE IS DEAD. AND HE WILL NEVER TAKE OUR LOVED ONES, AGAIN!
HURRAY!!!!
AND WE COULDN'T HAVE DONE IT, IF IT WASN'T FOR THE COURAGE AND BRAVERY OF YOUNG STEVE..
DAD, AND I COULDN'T HAVE DONE IT IF IT WASN'T FOR PIGGY.
OINK!

END OF VOLUME 1
COMING SOON...

VOLUME 2

THE SWAMP WITCH OF ENDOR

Manufactured by Amazon.ca
Bolton, ON

15237242R00019

This is the story of young Steve, who finds himself in an epic battle to save the lives of hundreds of villagers including his father. Battling zombies, skeletons, creepers, and the invincible Herobrine - will he be able to save his father and the hundreds of villagers from the curse Herobrine has placed on the land?

JUMP INTO THE ADVENTURE AND SEE FOR YOURSELF!

ISBN 9781494823313

90000 >

9 781494 823313